If Mr. Clean Calls, Tell Him I'm Not In!

If Mr. Clean Calls, Tell Him I'm Not In!

*A Look at Family Life
by Bob Hope's comedy writer*

Second Edition

MARTHA BOLTON

Fleming H. Revell
A Division of Baker Book House Co
Grand Rapids, Michigan 49516

Published by Fleming H. Revell
a division of Baker Book House Company
P.O. Box 6287, Grand Rapids, MI 49516-6287

Previously published 1989 by Regal Books, a division of GL Publications, Ventura, California.

Printed in the United States of America

Library of Congress Cataloging-in-Publication Data

Bolton, Martha, 1951–
    If Mr. Clean calls, tell him I'm not in! / Martha Bolton.
       p.   cm.
    ISBN 0-8007-5729-7 (paper)
    1. Family—Humor. 2. Family life—Humor. I. Title.
PN6231.F3B65   2000
818'.5402—dc21

00-024263

For current information about all releases from Baker Book House, visit our web site:
http://www.bakerbooks.com

In memory of my sister Linda
. . . with love

Contents

Foreword

SOMEONE has said, "You know it's going to be a bad day when your twin brother forgets your birthday." I suppose that's better than driving down the freeway behind a group of Hell's Angels when your horn gets stuck.

Martha Bolton takes a tongue-in-cheek look at common pressures like these. She helps us to see that the trouble with life is that it is so *daily*. She helps us to laugh and not cry under stress.

We all have experienced frustrating days and pressured schedules like those Martha writes about. I know I have felt like the Texan who rushed up to the airplane ticket counter and said, "Quick, give me a ticket."

"Where to?" asked the clerk.

"Anywhere," the Texan answered. "I've got business all over."

Martha Bolton knows that the good experiences in life and the not-so-good experiences happen to all people. Not everyone, however, looks at those events with positive eyes, as the author helps us learn to do.

Too many are like the pessimist who went duck hunting with the optimist. The optimist wanted to show the pessimist his new dog. When the first duck was shot, the optimist sent his dog to fetch the duck. The dog ran across the top of the water and brought back the duck. The pessimist said nothing. A second and third duck hit the lake, and the dog fetched them the same way—by running across the top of the water. Still, the pessimist did not respond. Finally, the optimist couldn't stand it any longer. He said, "Don't you see anything unusual about my new dog?"

"Yes," replied the pessimist, "he can't swim."

Although Martha sees the optimistic, humorous side of life, she is not afraid to poke fun at budgets and potlucks. She is even bold enough to take a humorous look at love and marriage. She would understand times like last week when my wife informed me that our car was flooded. "Where is it?" I asked.

"It's in the backyard in the swimming pool."

This doesn't mean that my wife and I don't get along. In fact, we have found the secret of a happy marriage. It's dinner out twice a week by candlelight and soft music. This is followed by a nice, slow walk home. (She eats out on Tuesdays and I eat out on Fridays.)

Martha helps us gain the perspective that God is there and he cares even when it's "One of Those Days." When the tough days come, I think of one of my favorite verses from the Bible. It is found in Luke 2:1: "And it came to pass in those days. . . ." And I'm sure glad it didn't come to stay.

I hope that you will enjoy this book as much as I did. I hope that it will help you to gain a positive perspective. May everyone laugh with you, instead of at you. And remember, you may not always be humorous, but you are funny.

Bob Phillips
Author of *The World's Greatest Collection of Clean Jokes*

Acknowledgments

I wish to thank:

My husband, Russ, who has recently developed a real interest in nutrition. Last night he said, "Stay out of the kitchen, dear."

My sons, Rusty, Matt, and Tony, who think the family dinner table is the corner booth at Dennys.

The Millie's Gang (they know who they are) for all the lunches and excuses to procrastinate.

And finally, to all of you across this great land who know the value of a good joke—but picked up this book anyway. I thank you. . . .

When Bad Days Happen to Good People

WHOEVER SAID TO STOP AND SMELL THE ROSES
OBVIOUSLY NEVER HAD A BEE FLY UP THEIR NOSE.

$\textsf{HAVE}$ you ever had one of those days when nothing seemed to go right?

√ Your alarm clock didn't go off. (Okay, maybe it did go off since it's now in pieces at the foot of your bed, but it didn't wake you up.)

√ Breakfast didn't turn out quite the way you expected. (You were hoping you'd only need *one* fire engine to put out the flames.)

√ You forgot to pick up your husband's suit at the cleaners and, as luck would have it, none of his ties match his bathrobe.

√ You got stuck in an elevator with four insurance salesmen and a guy who just picked up nine rolls of his vacation slides.

- √ The dog ate your son's science project and is now picking up cable TV. (And they're billing you for it.)
- √ You ran over something while backing out of your driveway. (Luckily, though, the police officer said he wasn't seriously injured.)
- √ Your grocery store shopping cart lost a wheel and they had to send for a tow cart to help you to the checkout counter.
- √ Your two-year-old decided to change his hairdo—he added his dinner to it.
- √ That slowpoke you tailgated and honked at for 15 miles turned out to be your pastor.
- √ You found out your name, address, and the precise time you eat dinner was just listed in the National Door-to-Door Salesmen's Directory.
- √ Your barber let his other customers use your scalp as a mirror.
- √ Your dentist informed you that he's got good news and bad news. The good news is he can fix your teeth. The bad news is they won't be in your mouth when he does it.

√ Your son rode his skateboard across your newly waxed floor four hours ago and still hasn't come in for a landing.

√ You pulled a muscle, sprained your wrist, and chipped a fingernail trying to twist the safety lid off your bottle of vitamins.

√ Your daughter brought home her new boyfriend and he was wearing enough metal to put U.S. Steel out of business.

√ Your car got a flat tire while being towed away for engine problems.

√ Your beautician made you sign a waiver stating you wouldn't sue if it still looked like you.

√ You called home to leave a message but got cut off by your own telephone answering machine.

√ Your kid called from college asking for more money. You send it, then realize you don't have a kid.

√ For the first time there's only one person in line in front of you at the bank . . . but he's robbing it.

√ You broke your ankle in your "Aerobics for Better Health" class.

√ Your paperboy threw your paper on a different, less accessible part of the roof.

√ You dropped your first aid kit on your foot, then got frostbite from the ice pack you put on it.

√ You got a "Let's do lunch!" invitation—from the IRS.

But even on days like this, isn't it nice to know our heavenly Father is with us? He can turn our vexations into victories, our trials into triumphs. We need only to trust him and remember when things go wrong, he has a way of making everything right again.

Dial-a-Pain

I DON'T MIND TALKING TO MACHINES.
SOMETIMES THEY'RE MORE INTERESTING THAN
THE REAL PEOPLE.

DON'T you love those direct-dialing telephone systems? That's where you call a place of business but instead of talking with a live operator, you're instructed to play push buttons with their machine until it eventually transfers your call to the person with whom you wish to speak.

A lot of department stores are using them. After a taped message thanking you for your call, the machine instructs you to press 2 if you want Sporting Goods, 4 if you want Small Appliances, and 9 if you don't really care what department you get, you just like pressing buttons.

Then, once you've coded in your desired department, the machine proceeds to ask more specific questions. If you want to know about a sale item, you're to press 3; if you have a problem with a product, you need to press 5; and if you wish to confess pulling the tags off all your mattresses, you'll need to press 7 and throw yourself on the mercy of Beautyrest.

Hospitals have begun using the direct-dialing system too. If you want the Emergency Room, you dial 1. Pediatrics? Dial 6. Dialing 8 gets you Respiratory Therapy, and for Medical Records, you dial 3. Of course, pitching the telephone against the wall will put your call directly through to the staff psychologist.

I could probably use a direct-dial system on my telephone—you know, for when the kids call. If they want Mom, they'd be instructed to press 8. If it's Dad they want, they can press 9. If they're going to be late for dinner, they press 6. If they need to be picked up, they press 5. If they want a raise in their allowance, they'd be instructed to hang up and try again later. If they want to borrow the car, they'd be told this number is no longer in service. And if it's report card day, they'd be asked to hold while their call is transferred to Dial-a-Prayer.

Actually, when you think about it, it's really not such a bad idea.

Happy Are the Parents
Whose Kids Are at Youth Camp

YOUTH CAMP: A PLACE WHERE PARENTS SEND
THEIR KIDS FOR A WEEK OF FUN AND RELAXATION
. . . THEIR OWN.

I remember the first time my children went off to youth camp. I worried so much, I couldn't eat. I couldn't sleep. I couldn't get that one question out of my mind: What if they come back early?

Actually, I did worry that weekend. I worried about a lot of things. I worried my children would have to sleep in dust-filled cabins and eat lousy food, and it would feel so much like home they'd never get homesick.

I worried about all the wild animals. What if a bear, snake, or coyote happened to wander into a cabin filled with a dozen or so young teenaged boys? Would the poor animal ever be the same again?

I worried about how big the forest was and how easy it would be to become separated from the rest of the group. But everyone assured me the counselors wouldn't get lost.

I prayed that weekend too.

I prayed the only souvenir my sons would bring home wouldn't be poison ivy. I prayed for our youth pastor who started out on the trip sane. I prayed he'd be able to return to society without an extensive rehabilitation program.

I prayed for our church bus driver that he'd not only have a safe trip up and back, but he'd retain most of his hearing as well.

I prayed that the boys would be free from harm, have a good time, and grow in the Lord.

But most of all, I prayed that their father and I would survive the weekend without them. After all, without any spats to referee, radios to turn down, or bathroom mirrors to wait in line in front of, what else would we have to do for fun?

Some Hang-Ups Are a Good Thing

MY TELEPHONE BILLS ARE SO THICK, THEY'VE
STARTED PRINTING THEM IN HARDBACK.

I don't think it's right for children to be on the telephone from morning 'til night. That's a mother's job.

All right, I confess, I do enjoy talking on the phone (I once did a book report on the Yellow Pages), but now that my children have started receiving their own calls, I hardly get near the instrument anymore.

Oh, I'm reasonably sure we still have a telephone. Why else would the phone company call me each month and thank me for keeping them in business?

And every once in a while I think I hear it ring. It's either the phone or the smoke alarm telling me dinner's ready.

There was a day when I could dial out anytime I wanted. I didn't have to take a number and wait for the receiver to be surgically removed from someone's hand.

I could also talk as long as I liked. I didn't have a teenager at my side bribing me with his month's allowance and, when the time comes, the nursing home of my choice if I'd clear the line.

Isn't it nice, though, that prayer doesn't work that way? We never have to wait for someone else to clear the line so we can talk to God. We can call him anytime of the day or night and we'll get through. No waiting. No busy signal. No problem.

If God Gave Speeding Tickets

AT OUR HOUSE, DINNER ISN'T SOMETHING WE
RUSH THROUGH. WE DON'T WANT IT HITTING OUR
BLOODSTREAM ANY SOONER THAN THE ANTIDOTE.

HAVE you ever found yourself wishing your microwave would hurry up?

Do you get impatient mixing your instant coffee?

The last time you stopped and smelled the roses, were they in a can of Glade?

Is your appointment calendar booked up into the afterlife?

Is your panting keeping the dog awake?

Have you ever thought of renting the space shuttle just so you can get all your errands done?

If you answered "yes" to any of the above (personally, I scored a five-out-of-six), then perhaps it's time to slow down on life's road and enjoy the trip a bit more.

Slowing down isn't easy, though. Life today seems permanently set in high gear. From the moment we wake up in the morning, we're driving the fast lane with no speed bumps in sight.

We eat in a hurry. I'm not saying how many fast-food restaurants I go to, but the other day I caught myself ordering into my mailbox and driving around the house.

We work in a hurry. We've got computers, FAX machines, call-waiting, beepers—and that's just for our preschoolers.

Our driving has speeded up, too. I'm amazed at how fast some people drive these days. No wonder you see signs that say "Speed checked by air-craft." It's the only way anyone can catch up to them.

At times, praying even gets rushed. We may get in such a hurry that we bow our heads and bring them up so fast we get whiplash.

We're in the age of instant breakfasts, 60-second hair conditioners, and drive-through surgical centers. We get our clothes cleaned in an hour and our printing done while we wait. We want it today, not tomorrow; this sec-ond, not this afternoon.

But why all the rush? Why not take a moment to let the coffee percolate? Why not tap the brakes a little and reevaluate what's really important in life?

Our only free day shouldn't be February 29 every other leap year, and our only stroll down the boulevard shouldn't be when we run out of gas. After all, the world God created isn't spinning any faster. So why should his children?

The Family Vacation or Fifty Ways to Answer "Are We There Yet?"

NO MATTER WHERE YOUR FAMILY VACATION
TAKES YOU, FOR ALL OF US THE FIRST
DESTINATION IS ALWAYS THE SAME—
HOME AGAIN TO GET WHATEVER IT IS
WE'VE FORGOTTEN.

EACH year you know it's coming. You try to prepare for it. You try to brace yourself for it. But no matter what you do, it seems you're never quite ready for . . . the family vacation.

Family vacations, though, do have their plus side. They give you time to get to know one another again, time to communicate. I know whenever our family goes on a vacation, the communication begins the moment we pull out of the driveway. My husband is usually the first to open up.

"Uh, dear," he'll begin. "Why are we towing a six-foot U-Haul trailer full of suitcases when we're only going to be staying *four* days?"

"You're absolutely right, dear. I really should have rented the truck."

"But the only things you left behind were the carpets."

"That's not true," I'll answer. "What do you think I used for padding?"

The communication takes a different turn a few minutes down the road.

"Sweetheart," he says with a smile, "did you remember to turn off the sprinklers?"

"You never told me to turn off the sprinklers."

"Well, did you check to see if all the burners were turned off?"

"No, but don't worry. If the house catches on fire, the sprinklers will put it out."

For some reason that's never a good enough answer, and inevitably he'll announce, "I'm turning around. We're going back to check."

"Going back?" the kids grumble from the rear seat.

"But, Dad, the neighbors will call the fire department if they see smoke coming out of our windows."

"Not necessarily. They'll probably just think your mother's cooking again."

And so, we go back. We always go back. In fact, my youngest son once wrote a school paper on "How I Spent My Summer Vacation Making U-Turns in Front of My House."

After a quick recheck of the homestead, we'll continue on our trip and the communication resumes. It's the children's turn now to share their innermost feelings.

"Aren't we there yet?"

"Aw, man, when are we going to get there?"

"He's kicking me!"

"Am not!"

"Are too!"

"Dad, what does it mean when a policeman turns his red lights on behind you?"

This openness continues throughout the remainder of the trip.

"How come he always gets to sit by the window?"

"Can you turn the radio up louder? I still have some of my hearing left."

"What do you mean, the Grand Canyon doesn't have a roller coaster?"

Amazingly enough, though, by the time a family vacation is over, we really have grown a little closer. My husband and I can truthfully say we've opened up more to the children—his wallet, my purse, our credit card holder. And the children haven't held back sharing their aspirations, their goals—like, "Now can we go home?"

Yes, a family vacation can be a wonderful thing. Just make sure you schedule a second vacation to rest up from it.

The Backseat Driver's Hall of Fame

IN LOS ANGELES, MERGING TRAFFIC
HAS COME TO MEAN EXCHANGING BUMPERS.

IF ever there's a Backseat Driver's Hall of Fame, I'll no doubt be the first inductee. I take my backseat driving seriously. I tell my husband when he needs to drive faster, drive slower, turn right, turn left, make a U-turn, or park. And he appreciates it. After all, he knows I'm better behind the wheel than he is. Why else is he always saying that when he goes to the funny farm, I'll be the one driving him there?

When you get right down to it, though, men are far worse backseat drivers than women. My husband continually criticizes me for my three-point turns. He doesn't think two of the points should involve tow trucks. He never seems satisfied with the way I park, either. For some reason, he's of the opinion our car should retain some of its paint when I do it. And I don't know why, but my husband is always nagging at me not to stop on railroad tracks. Doesn't he realize that, with that train coming, I can't hear him anyway?

Still, no matter how well intentioned backseat driving is, it's probably best to leave the decisions to the person who has the keenest perspective of the situation—the person behind the wheel. The person in control.

This is true of life, also. Sometimes we may find ourselves trying to backseat drive with God. We tell him when we think his answer is too slow. We

wonder why he's chosen this route instead of that one. Or we try to find our own shortcuts, only to have them turn into dead ends.

How much better would it be if we merely placed our trust in his judgment? After all, who best to have sitting behind the wheel guiding our lives than the one who knows the road better than any of us? In other words, maybe we need to relax a little more and leave the driving to him.

The Budget Balancing Act

8

REMEMBER WHEN "CHARGE" WAS A MILITARY
TERM INSTEAD OF A CONSUMER ONE, AND LEFT
A LOT FEWER CASUALTIES BEHIND?

EVERY family ought to have a budget—a list that shows exactly what you'll need to borrow from American Express to pay off your VISA card so you can use it to charge your MasterCard payment so you'll be below your limit and can use that to charge your Discovery and Diner's Club bills.

A family budget, however, isn't the easiest thing to agree upon. Whenever my husband and I try to make one out, he will inevitably propose all the cutbacks in my spending alone. He will made ridiculous demands like, "Don't buy so much from the Avon lady that she has to airlift your order to our porch." He will insist I throw away my I.D. bracelet that says, "If found, please return me to the nearest mall." He will even recommend the phone company come out and disconnect my private line to QVC.

Eventually, though, we do come to a compromise on what the spending cuts should be, and for the most part, we try to adhere to them. These days you have to. The cost of living is too high not to budget your money.

For one thing, the price of food has skyrocketed. Nowadays, when you ring for a butcher, it's not to cut your meat. It's for a loan application.

Clothing costs have risen dramatically, too. I can remember a time when house dresses didn't come with a mortgage, and buying a business suit didn't mean you had to sell the business.

And have you looked at the cost of housing lately? Sure, a man's home is his castle, but should the king and queen have to get second and third jobs just to pay for it?

Still, even with the mounting prices and tightened budgets, isn't it nice to relax in the knowledge that if we trust in the Lord, he will meet our every need? And he doesn't even charge interest.

My Love Is Like a Red, Red Nose

9

I'M CONVINCED A LOT OF WOMEN END UP IN DIVORCE COURT NOT BECAUSE THEY WANT TO LEAVE THEIR HUSBANDS. THEY'RE JUST LOOKING FOR A WARM ROOM.

WHEN my husband stopped our wedding ceremony to adjust the chapel thermostat, I should have known then what kind of life I was destined to lead with him—especially since I had already adjusted it to my liking on my way down the aisle.

Frankly, I think engaged couples should be given a climatic-compatibility test before taking that big plunge into matrimony.

Over the past nineteen years of marriage, I don't think my husband and I have ever agreed on what temperature to keep the house. He prefers it on the cooler side—meaning I can make block ice in my kitchen sink. I, on the other hand, prefer life in a warmer environment. I visit Death Valley only when I want to cool off.

With a determined effort on both our parts, however, we have managed to find several ways to compromise. When he opens the windows, I turn up the heat. When he turns on the air conditioner, I light all the burners on the kitchen stove. And when he sets his side of the electric blanket to "Night of the Glacier," I know that's my cue to turn my side up to a more suitable setting (somewhere between "The San Francisco Fire" and "Evening at Three Mile Island").

Another way we've found to compromise is for me to dress warmer around the house—you know, ski jacket, fur-lined boots, lead apron. This works out all right, but it tends to get a little heavy in the shower.

That compromise is the key to a happy marriage is something I've come to realize. It doesn't matter if he has the house so cold I can make ice sculptures out of my breath, or if I've got it so hot even the dog's trying to take off its coat. All that matters is being together. And my husband agrees. It really does go back to our wedding day. Even though we competed for control of the thermostat, and when it came time to lift the veil, I told him to put it back down, he was letting in a draft, we've never let any of this come between us. After all, when we said, "I do," it was for all temperatures 'til death by heatstroke or frostbite do us part.

Chicken Salad for the Soul

10

I'M NOT THAT GREAT OF A COOK. FOR YEARS MY
FAMILY THOUGHT MOLD WAS A FROSTING.

WHICH dish is yours, Mom?"

Now, there's a question my children have never asked at a church potluck. They know exactly which dish is mine. That's because they have been briefed ahead of time and have received their instructions.

You see, the rule of our house is that each family member is to spot my dish on the serving table and take a minimum of two scoops. Any brave family member willing to go the extra mile and take three scoops gets an additional hour on their play time and first dibs on the Pepto-Bismol.

All of this is necessary, of course, to make sure the dish I've slaved over, the dish I've worked all night on, the dish I've proudly prepared, doesn't—as in years past—get mistaken for the scraps bowl.

Now, I'll admit, most of my cooking leaves something to be desired (namely, a stomach pump and notification of the partaker's next of kin), but it still hurts to watch church member after church member walk past my culinary masterpiece without slowing down a beat. In fact, some of the flies even seem to take the long way around just to avoid it.

I've often wished I could cook like those women whose dishes disappear two minutes after they set them out. It never fails that hungry attendees will be scraping the bottom of their pans while my casserole just sits there and spoils.

In fact, in all the years I've been potlucking, I can recall only one time when my dish disappeared quickly. But, unfortunately, no one's needed a doorstop since.

I suppose when you get right down to it, I can't really blame the folks for passing on my cooking. It's just that when they do, I have to take it back home with me, which creates another problem:

Do you have any idea how much crane companies charge these days?

Stalked by a Computer

11

CREDIT CARD—THE LEGAL DEVICE USED TO
CHARGE YOU 20 PERCENT INTEREST ON MONEY
YOU WON'T BE EARNING UNTIL TOMORROW TO BUY
THINGS YOU DON'T NEED TODAY.

$I F$ you've ever had a disagreement with a computer over the slightest billing error, you know the battle usually goes something like this:

Computer, letter dated October 30
Dear Valued Customer:

We hate to mention this, but as of this date we have not received your payment. Won't you kindly send your remittance at your earliest convenience?

Again, we are sorry to bother you. We trust you will take this letter in the tone it was intended.

Thank you, and have a nice day.

Customer, letter dated November 6
Dear Sir:

I mailed my payment for $35 on October 1. A copy of the canceled check is enclosed. Kindly adjust your records accordingly.

Thank you.

Computer, letter dated November 20, stamped
URGENT—READ AT ONCE

Dear Mrs. Past-Due:

Credit is a valuable thing. Most people want to do everything they can to protect their good credit. So, why don't you?

Since you have ignored our first letter and have not sent in your payment, your credit privileges are now in jeopardy.

Won't you please get with it and send in your check for $35 today?

Thank you, and have a nice day.

Customer, letter dated November 26

Dear Sir:

Don't you read your mail? I sent you my check #543 on October 1. I also sent you a copy of my canceled check cashed by you on October 8.

I am now enclosing another copy for your reference, and I would appreciate your immediate crediting of my account.

Thank you.

Computer, letter dated December 4, written in red ink
DEAR MADAM:

SINCE YOU HAVE CONTINUED TO IGNORE OUR PREVIOUS REQUESTS FOR PAYMENT, YOU LEAVE US NO ALTERNATIVE OTHER THAN TO TAKE FURTHER ACTION TO PROTECT OUR INTERESTS.

WE FEEL WE HAVE GIVEN YOU AMPLE OPPORTUNITY TO MAKE GOOD YOUR DELINQUENCY. BUT YOU HAVE MADE NO EFFORT WHATSOEVER TO COMMUNICATE WITH US. IT'S CLODS LIKE YOU WITH OUTSTANDING DEBTS WHO DRIVE THE COST OF LIVING OUT OF SIGHT. HOW DID WE EVER GIVE YOU CREDIT IN THE FIRST PLACE?

YOUR CLEAN RECORD AND GOOD CREDIT RATING MAY HAVE FOOLED US AT FIRST, BUT NOW WE'VE GOT YOUR NUMBER, YOU FLAKE! AND YOU CAN REST ASSURED WE'RE GOING TO INFORM ALL THE CREDIT BUREAUS ABOUT THIS SO YOU CAN'T PULL YOUR LITTLE SCHEME ON ANYBODY ELSE.

However, since you have been a good customer in the past, we're going to give you until December 5 to send us your check, which, by the time you receive this, was probably yesterday.

We hope you take this letter in the tone it was intended. Thank you, and have a nice day.

Customer, letter dated December 9
Dear Sir:

Now you're beginning to get on my nerves. I have paid the bill in question. I have sent you two copies of the canceled check. A third one is enclosed.

So, please, quit sending me bills!

Computer Mailgram, dated December 20
Dear Parasite:

Because of your good record, we have tried to be lenient. We have tried to be fair. But we don't even like you anymore.

You continue to ignore our letters, and now we have no choice. Your credit privileges have been revoked, and our representatives have all been issued your picture and the names of your family members.

The next correspondence you receive will be from our collection agency. Watch for it . . . and have a nice day.

Collection agency jerk-gram, dated December 25
Merry Christmas!

Allow us to introduce ourselves. We are a collection agency. We make our living collecting from jerks like you.

You have until midnight tonight to deck our halls with your payment, or we deck you.

Do we make ourselves clear?

Thank you, and have a nice day.

Customer telegram, dated December 25
Dear Sir:

I don't believe this. I've paid you, you've cashed my check, I've sent you three copies of the canceled check, but you continue to ignore my letters.

Now it's fight-back time. I'm calling in Ralph Nader, the Better Business Bureau, and my congressman. When they get through with you, you'll be sorry.

Computer, letter dated January 3
Dear Valued Customer:
Thank you for your payment.

Your credit has been reinstated and, as one of our valued customers, we are happy to inform you that your credit line has been increased.

Why put off all those things you've been wanting to buy? Come in today and just say, "Charge it." We'll bill you later. It's as simple as that.

So remember, just say, "Charge it" and your worries are over.

Thank you, and do have a nice day.

All I can say is, aren't you glad our prayers to God aren't handled by a computer?

Mirror, Mirror on the Wall, When Did My Cheeks Begin to Fall?

12

I DON'T BOTHER WITH TANNING BEDS. I JUST WAIT FOR MY LIVER SPOTS TO CONNECT.

I'VE never considered myself photogenic. Oh, I take a nice picture every once in a while—when the lens cap is left on. And I look great in group shots. (Hands Across America was my best one yet.) But close-up pictures of me generally leave a lot to be desired—like distance.

So, you can well imagine my excitement when I discovered a photographer who would not only take my portrait but would first give me a complete makeover. Considering his special makeup, hairstyling, and lighting, I figured I had to come away with at least one good shot.

With visions of a poster-worthy finished product, I excitedly made an appointment. Creating a new me, however, wasn't going to be easy. On the morning of my photo session, I awoke with so many pillow creases on my face I couldn't tell if I was looking at my cheeks or a map of the California fault system. And there were enough bags under my eyes to put Hefty out of business. Still, I kept the faith and went.

The makeover began with a camouflaging foundation. This was to hide any blemishes, liver spots, or skin discolorations I might have. They applied it with a spray gun.

Next came the challenge of finding a base makeup closest to my natural skin color, which ended up being a cross between "Clown White" and "Anemic Glory."

Now, it was time to add some color to my cheeks. After debating between a soft rose, a deep pink, and a blood transfusion, he made the decision to go with the rose.

With eye shadows, mascara, and eyeliner, he was able to make my eyes look bigger and brighter, and he also managed to accomplish something I've never been able to do before. He made them look like a matched set.

With a special lip brush, he redefined my lips, giving them the more traditional horizontal look.

It was time now for my hair. He fluffed it up, pulled it over, teased it mercilessly, and basically gave it a fullness even Don King doesn't enjoy.

After approximately an hour and a half (he didn't even charge extra for overtime), I was a new person. I looked fifteen years younger. The bags had disappeared, the fault lines were gone. I looked healthy, vibrant. The transformation was amazing. Of course, if I smiled my cheeks would crack and my forehead would crumble into my lap, but I was a new person.

All in all, it was a fun day, but the best part was when I was able to get home and comb out my hair, chisel off my makeup, and get back to being myself again. Being very nearly glamorous was nice, but what's nicer is knowing God loves me just the way I am.

The Family That Wheezes Together ...

13

I TRIED WORKING OUT ON A TREADMILL,
BUT MY PILLOW KEPT GETTING STUCK IN
THE CONVEYOR BELT.

I believe it's a good idea for families to exercise together. That way, when Mom collapses, there'll be someone there to call the paramedics.

My family and I have tried several means of group exercise. We've gone through obstacle courses together. (It's the only way to get from one end of our house to the other.)

Family basketball games are fun, too, although I often get called for traveling. Not just a step or two. I usually travel all the way to the snack bar.

We've also organized a few family baseball games, but they make me run the bases in order, so what fun is that?

Exhilarating, challenging, push-to-the-limit sort of hikes are something we try to do on a regular basis. They're beginning to get too rough for me, though. Lately, everyone's been wanting to go beyond our driveway.

We've even joined a health club together. There, Dad spends his time lifting weights, the kids will usually opt for racquetball, and I'll try to swim at least four laps a visit. I could probably do more laps, but it's not that easy to turn around in a Jacuzzi.

Yet, with all the importance of getting physical exercise together, it's even more important for a family to exercise its spiritual muscles together. Reading the Bible and praying as a unit builds spiritual endurance and strength. And staying in shape in that department is one of the best things a family can do.

If Mr. Clean Calls,
Tell Him I'm Not In!

14

I SERVE LEFTOVERS THE EASY WAY. I NEVER
CLEAR THE TABLE.

I hate housework. I only do it when it's absolutely necessary—like when I can't find one of the kids. Or when the floral pattern on my bedsheets starts taking root.

There are other signs I watch for that let me know it's time to clean the house. For instance, when I find snow at the top of my dirty clothes pile, I know wash day is at hand. Or when a rude guest signs in on my coffee table with her fingers, I concede it might be time to drag out the Pledge. And when my Airwick Solid melts 15 minutes after I set it out, I figure it's probably trying to tell me something.

Yet, even though I'm the only woman in the world who owns a washing machine with a mildew cycle, I still realize housekeeping is a necessary part of life. Boarding up the shower is no way to get rid of unsightly lime stains, and the dishwasher overflowing shouldn't be a prerequisite to mopping the kitchen floor.

It's just that I don't want to overdo it. You know, like those people whose houses smell of so much Lysol, every time you take a breath you disinfect your lungs. These people are so clean and tidy, you couldn't have archaeological digs on their dresser tops. They'd never have so many dishes on their kitchen sink they forget what color it is. And pest exterminators would never consider using their homes for training maneuvers.

I prefer to think the perfect housekeeper is someone who can strike a happy medium. It's like the old saying, "A home should be clean enough to be healthy, but dirty enough to be happy."

Or to put it another way, "Keep your floors clean enough to eat off of, but leave enough food there to make it worth your while!"

I Don't Care If It Is Cool. You Are *Not* Shampooing Your Hair with the Easter Egg Dye!

WHEN GOD CREATED ADAM AND EVE, YOU'LL NOTICE HE SKIPPED THE TEENAGE YEARS.

15

I think someone should come out with a "Parent's Guide to Cool." It would be sort of a reference tool that parents could refer to when trying to decide whether their offspring are merely dressing with the times or whether something did, in fact, explode in their closet.

Parents should not be expected to keep up with what's in and what's out, what's chic and what's geek. How can we know if our children's hair in rainbow colors is intentional or if it's from a severe vitamin deficiency requiring medical attention? How are we supposed to know if jeans with ripped knees are in style or merely the result of a moth on a high-fiber denim diet?

Naturally, the guidebook would need to be updated on a regular basis. Fads change quickly. The other day I bought an outfit that went out of style before the clerk could put it into the bag.

It might also be helpful if the guidebook included a Dictionary of Cool Talk. This is so we'll be able to understand what language it is that our teens are speaking instead of automatically assuming too much mousse has seeped in through their scalp and is now affecting their brain.

There is a market for such a book, but until someone sees fit to publish it, I guess parents are on their own.

To be perfectly honest, though, I haven't really minded the wrinkled look, the torn look, or even the faded look. After all, I haven't had to say, "Why don't you take better care of your clothes?" for years.

What Do You Mean, Pizza-Man Doesn't Deliver Here?

16

I LOVE CAMPING. IT'S THE ONLY TIME MY FAMILY
DOESN'T COMPLAIN ABOUT THE DIRT IN THE FOOD.

I suppose I should have known when my husband bought camping equipment several years ago, he'd expect me to escape with him every once in a while to the great outdoors.

But I'm not the camping type. I'll go camping when Coleman makes a microwave and tents start coming with "Best Western" signs. You see, taking a shower under a two-foot faucet and spraying insect repellent on so thick I gain four pounds is not my idea of a vacation. I don't like dirt in my food, bugs in my drink, or rocks in my bed. If I wanted all that, I'd just stay home. I don't like the crowds either. I'm not into elbow-to-elbow fishing, mob hiking, or taking in the scenic view of 400 RVs. Nor do I enjoy using barbecue pits on the time-share program.

Still, every so often I lose the family-vacation vote and have to go.

Take, for instance, last summer. I cast my vote for Hawaii. My husband (and savings account) voted for a week of camping. The kids voted for camping too, citing how much they enjoyed watching me cook over a blazing fire. I reminded them that was how I cooked all our meals (around our house "variable low cloudiness" has come to mean "soup's on"), but it was no use. Before I knew it, we were pulling into a campground my husband had seen advertised in *Mosquito Travel* magazine.

"This is it?" I grumbled, surveying the tumbleweeds.

"Isn't it great?" my husband exclaimed, taking in the view from the highest point of the camp—an anthill.

"This is it?" I repeated.

He nodded proudly.

"But isn't that a chemical dump site over there on the other side of that fence?" I asked, pointing off in the distance.

Pretending he didn't hear me, he mumbled something about it getting dark, then asked me to assist him with our new "easy set-up" tent.

Now, setting up an "easy set-up" tent requires only three things: skill, patience, and the telephone number of a nearby Ramada Inn, just in case.

You may not realize it, but the words "easy set-up" are merely code words for "You ain't ever gonna get this put together, sucker!" In fact, that's why they always include a picture of the tent along with the directions. It's so you can see what the tent would have looked like had you not given up on it and thrown it into the lake.

After four hours of "easy set-up," my husband finally finished our canvas abode. It leaned eight different directions (none of them upright). And that wasn't the only problem. We couldn't zip the door shut either. Every time we tried, the window would fly open. Then, if we managed to shut both the door and the window, the roof would collapse.

Too tired to battle it any longer, we decided to leave well enough alone and sleep with the door open. If a wild animal happened to wander in during the night, all I knew was he wasn't getting my pillow.

Before long, everyone was asleep. Everyone but me, that is. I couldn't get to sleep because of all the night sounds—you know, crickets, owls, the rock band practicing in the next tent over. (I'm not saying how loud it was, but when was the last time you saw squirrels stuffing nuts in their ears?)

It didn't really matter, though, because, since we had pitched our tent in the dark, we unknowingly set it on top of an automatic sprinkler, and it was just a matter of time before we'd all have to get up anyway.

Morning found me dressed and ready to start cooking breakfast. They say there's nothing quite like waking up to the aroma of bacon sizzling over an open fire, so I quickly woke up my family so they could enjoy it coming from the other campsites before I started cooking.

There was, though, a positive side to my campfire delicacies. While all the other campers had to put up with hundreds of bees buzzing around their food, my food drew only the ones with nothing to live for.

Still, all in all, the week wasn't that bad. We got to tell stories around the campfire, go for long hikes, and basically enjoy each other away from the fast pace of big city life. And even though I had so many bites I felt like a club med for mosquitoes, I realize it's important to get away from it all every once in a while, to rough it, to go without modern conveniences.

And, yes, I have to admit, I'd do it all over again—but next time, I'm finding a campground with valet parking and room service.

Some Assembly Required (and a Little Prozac Wouldn't Hurt Either)

17

ASSEMBLY INSTRUCTIONS: THAT CRUMPLED UP PIECE OF PAPER YOU TAKE OUT OF THE TRASH CAN WHEN ALL ELSE FAILS.

I remember the Christmas my husband and I bought a new bicycle for one of our boys. Our son was thrilled, excited, elated. But then, right in the midst of all the merriment, something happened to ruin the moment. He asked us to put it together.

I tried to get him just to play with the parts for a month or so, but he wasn't interested. I ripped the picture of the bike off the carton and told him to straddle that for a while. He merely shook his head. He wanted the bike itself, the real thing. And he wanted it to look exactly like the photo.

So, my husband grabbed his toolbox, I grabbed some aspirin, and we began. We labored. We sweated. We worked into the night. Finally, we got the box open. Then came the real fun—that of trying to decipher the instructions that were written in a hardback trilogy and had more steps than the Taj Mahal.

They did promise, though, that the only tools we would need would be a screwdriver, a hammer, and an adjustable wrench. But, by the time we were done, we had used every tool in the garage *except* the screwdriver, hammer, and adjustable wrench. (Although, at times, several uses for the hammer did cross our minds.)

After six hours of trying to get A into B, connect D to F, slide G through H while bypassing E altogether until Step #9 (at which point we were to overlap H with I), we finally completed our project. The handlebars were on sideways, the kickstand kicked back, and there were six screws unaccounted for, but we were done.

"But it doesn't look anything like the picture," my son moaned.

"Sure, it does," I assured him. Then, snatching the picture from his hands, I cut it into tiny pieces, scrambled them to match up with the contraption we had just built, and smiled confidently. "See, now it looks *exactly* like the picture."

"Maybe we should take it back to the store and get some help," my son said. "You know, from the people who made the bike in the first place. They'll know how to put it together."

I had to agree. I'm sure the guy who designed the bike didn't mean for both wheels to be on the same side or the seat to be pointing heavenward.

So we took the bike back to the store and, within minutes, they had it looking and operating precisely as it was meant to. It was beautiful. Our son was thrilled, and my husband and I were in awe of how simple a task it was for someone who knew what he was doing. After all, who better to put a bike together than its maker?

Sometimes we may need a little help assembling our lives, too. No matter how hard we try, we just can't seem to make A fit into B. We work at it and work at it, but it doesn't end up looking anything like it was supposed to. That's when it's time to gather up all the pieces and take them to the Lord. After all, who better to put a life together than its maker?

Shedding a Few Tons

18

I KEEP SO MANY STACKS OF PAPER AROUND
MY HOUSE, MY HUSBAND HOLDS MONTHLY
AVALANCHE DRILLS.

EVERY once in a while (in a moment of delirium), I decide it's time to clear out the clutters in my home—not just move them from one end of the house to the other. I mean, really clear them out.

I begin by giving away those stacks and stacks of magazines I haven't gotten around to reading yet—you know, the ones I ordered thinking I'd win my name on a check for ten million dollars, but all I got my name on was a mailing list.

Next, it's my old clothes that go. The basic rule of thumb here is, if the moths have been seen in it more than I have, it gets the heave-ho.

Old toys and worn-out games aren't safe from my anti-clutter mood, either. After all, what good is a Monopoly game if all the properties are on the verge of being condemned?

I usually hit the closets next, leaving a trail, of course, in case I can't find my way back out. When I go into the kids' closets, I leave a will as well.

The final clutter haven I tackle is under the beds. I'm not saying what excitement that task holds in store for me, but two episodes of "Wild Animal Kingdom" were filmed under there.

But once all the work is done and the clutters have been cleared away, the house does seem a little fresher, a little cleaner, a little more livable.

From time to time, we may notice our lives becoming cluttered, too. We find ourselves hanging on to things we should have tossed out years ago. We've got this shoved in that corner, that shoved in this corner, and this tucked away down here. It's then that we probably need to stop and clear out just a little more room for the Lord.

ROLAIDS—THEY'RE NOT JUST FOR BREAKFAST
ANYMORE.

IT'S important for families to eat together. That's why I've instructed my children that they are in no way to grab a microwave pizza from the freezer or make themselves a bologna sandwich just before dinner time. After all, if their father and I have to sit down to a home-cooked meal, why shouldn't they?

Besides, the family dinner table is more than a testing ground for Rolaids. It's a place where families can discuss the day's events.

"Your teacher called this afternoon. She said you haven't disrupted the class all week."

"See, I told you I've been trying to behave."

"I know. And being absent all week didn't hurt, either."

Dad's work is discussed next.

"I think the boss is really impressed with me."

"Really? What makes you say that, dear?"

"Well, why else is he always saying, 'What'd I do to deserve him?'"

My day is discussed, too.

"You won't believe who I ran into today."

"An old friend?"

"No. A new Toyota."

But eating together renders something even more important than conversation. It gives a feeling of closeness, a sense of "family."

When it's just the family, we don't have to go into the garage and bring out that extra stool or drag over the piano bench for someone to sit on. There's already a chair reserved for each member. There's a place set for us. We belong.

It's the same in the family of God. We don't have to eat from TV trays or stand off in the corner. There's a chair already reserved for us at his table. There's a place set just for us. We belong.

From "Endless Love" to "Romancing the Stone"

20

YOU KNOW THE ROMANCE HAS GONE OUT OF YOUR MARRIAGE WHEN THE LAST TIME HE SAID "BABE" WAS WHEN THAT PIG MOVIE WAS GETTING READY TO COME ON.

I'LL never forget the year my husband gave car mats to me for our anniversary. And as if that wasn't breathtaking enough, he later took me to a very classy restaurant for dinner—you know, one of those places where you're not allowed to honk in their drive-through lane. That was the same year I wrapped up a Weedwhacker and a bunion file for his gifts.

And who says romance is dead?

Recently, though, we've come to realize you've got to work at keeping a marriage fresh and exciting. If the only reason you dim the lights is to get the glare off the television screen, and the only cuddling you're doing is when the heater breaks down in your car, then perhaps it's time to work a little harder at maintaining that "first-love" relationship.

When my husband and I first met, my heart fluttered. His heart fluttered. Now when our hearts flutter, we just take an antacid.

Back then, we made sure we looked our best for each other, too. He had to have every hair in place and I had to look as though I had just stepped off the cover of *Vogue* magazine (or at least the first couple of pages).

After a few comfortable years of marriage, however, all that's changed. Oh, he still keeps every hair in place, but it really doesn't take that much time to mousse the two of them. And these days, I look more like I stepped off the cover of *Bathrobes Quarterly*.

That's why we agreed to start giving our marriage the attention it deserves. We're doing things to nurture it, pamper it, and ensure its longevity.

For one thing, we're spending more evenings in front of a warm, crackling fire—only now it's in the fireplace, not in the kitchen. I don't let little things bother me anymore, either—like snoring. I bought some earplugs and now my husband says he can't even hear me.

You see, we realize that for a marriage to stay healthy it has to be watered, pruned, and cared for.

Sometimes, we fall short of giving our relationship with the Lord the attention it deserves, too. As in a marriage, it's easy to begin taking his love for granted, to become complacent in our walk with him. And, just as in a marriage, we may need to stop from time to time and get back into that first-love relationship with him.

Are You *Sure* the Wise Men Wore Turtlenecks?

21

I'VE NEVER BEEN MUCH OF A SEAMSTRESS.
I WAS THE ONLY ONE IN MY SEWING CLASS WHO
HAD TO WEAR A FULL BODY THIMBLE.

remember the year my pastor put me in charge of making the costumes for the Christmas pageant. He and the church board felt I was the perfect person for the job. In other words, I wasn't at the planning meeting.

Now, I'll be the first to admit that sewing has never been one of my talents. The blouse that I made in high school is still on display there showing how *not* to sew on sleeves. (Evidently there's some unwritten rule about attaching only two.)

But not wanting to disappoint the cast, I agreed to give it my best shot.

I finished the shepherd costumes first and, except for the one with the turtleneck and fringe, they turned out rather authentic looking.

To my astonishment, I succeeded with the angel costumes as well. A few of them had a little more material than they needed (they could have been an ark cover for Noah), but they worked out fine for the play.

Herod's costume was a cinch, although while pinning it on, I stuck the poor actor so many times he should have been awarded a Purple Heart.

The wise men's robes turned out exceptionally nice also—once I remembered to put in the holes for their heads to go through.

Finally all the costumes were sewn, the cast looked terrific, and I couldn't have been prouder as I sat in the audience that night enjoying the pageant just like every other parent—with an instamatic, a Polaroid, and a video camera.

I learned a valuable lesson that evening too. I learned that when the Lord gives us something to do, we should do it. Even when we don't feel qualified for the job, if we'll only trust him, he will make it work out just fine.

As a matter of fact, I've already volunteered to sew the new choir robes for our church. And as soon as the pastor quits changing his phone number, I can get the go-ahead to start.

Guest of Honor

22

OPTIMIST: SOMEONE WHO, AS THE AIRPLANE IS CRASHING, SAYS, "OH, GOOD, FINALLY THERE'S NO LINE AT THE RESTROOM!"

NOT long ago, it became necessary to replace our old dining room set. It was beginning to sag in the middle (from years of holding up my biscuits, no doubt), and it bore numerous knife marks and scratches (from dinner guests who had opted for the easier task of cutting through it instead of my meatloaf).

In its place we bought a new French provincial dining table along with six chairs, two leaves, and a shine you could tan by. It was beautiful. Day after day, week after week, I'd walk past it admiringly. My husband would comment on how nice it looked. My children were even impressed.

Then, the inevitable came. One day, my eldest son asked if we were ever planning to eat off it or were we merely saving it for a souvenir.

He had a point.

I don't know why it is, but too often we tend to save our best and newest things for company.

My good china is in my buffet collecting dust while the family and I eat off designer Dixieware.

My fine crystal is in boxes shoved in a cupboard while we drink out of souvenir Slurpee cups from 7-Eleven.

I even have brand-new bedsheets that I've been saving for guests. Meanwhile, my husband and I get the ones that only fit when I roll up our mattress like a croissant.

But my son's comment that day reminded me it doesn't have to be like that. After all, what dinner guests could be more important to me than my own family?

So, right then and there, I determined things were going to be different. I was going to treat my family to a very special "company" type meal (you know, where you use forks).

This time, when my son walked by the table, he looked at his crystal-clear reflection in the china, which I had meticulously placed around the table, and naturally inquired, "How does my hair look?"

Then he went on to ask, "Someone special coming for dinner tonight, Mom?"

I nodded.

"You're looking at him."

What's That Silence I Hear?

PARENTS NEED TO GET OUT ONCE IN A WHILE WITHOUT THE KIDS. THERE'S A LIMIT TO HOW LONG ONE SHOULD WEAR EARPLUGS.

WITH today's fast-paced living it's easy for parents to forget what it's like to go out for a night on the town. We forget there's more to life than eating kiddie meals out of space saucers. There's an adult world out there waiting to be discovered—a place where you eat off real plates and where "preferred seating" means a booth with a view instead of a counter with saddle seats and stirrups.

It does exist, and sometimes we owe it to ourselves and to our families to get away from the McHustle-McBustle of life and find it.

I recall one particular evening when my husband decided it was time to do just that. He made reservations at one of the most expensive restaurants in our town. It was the type of establishment that didn't honor coupons or give out game tokens, and the only arches it had were in the maitre d's Gucci shoes. I couldn't wait.

We arrived at the restaurant about fifteen minutes early for our 7:00 P.M. reservations and followed the valet parking arrows to the front entrance.

"Now, this is real class," I said in wide-eyed appraisal. "They're even going to park our car."

"Not ours," my husband said with a frown. "The valet appears to be waving us on."

"Why didn't you bring the good car?" I grumbled.

"This *is* the good car," he said as we stalled out trying to make it over a speed bump.

Once inside, we were able to relax and just enjoy the ambiance, and there was plenty of it to enjoy. The menu didn't have pictures, the tablecloth didn't stick to our arms from dried catsup spills, and the waiter didn't even know what a booster seat was. In fact, he gagged when I inadvertently ordered chocolate milk.

"Look! They even give party hats," I exclaimed, pinning one to my hair.

"Those aren't party hats," my husband said, snatching it off my head. "They're our napkins. They fold them that way."

All in all, though, it was nice to get out and enjoy the finer side of life for a change, to be somewhere where we didn't have to eat out of Styrofoam or listen to little ones crying.

As a matter of fact, the only crying I did have to listen to was my husband's—when the check came.

How to Keep a Song in Your Heart—
Even When a Few Sour Notes
Come Your Way

I DON'T GET IT. I'M IN A PROTESTANT CHOIR, BUT
THE DIRECTOR KEEPS ASKING ME TO TAKE A VOW
OF SILENCE.

LIFE is so much easier when you go through it with a song in your heart. No matter what comes your way, you can usually find the perfect song to help get you through it.

For instance, when you're driving down the freeway, twenty minutes late for Sunday school, try singing, "Hold the Fort for I Am Coming!"

When you're hosting a birthday party for thirty rambunctious six-year-olds, humming "Blessed Quietness" just might help. And when they decide to turn it into a slumber party? Try "Hasten Thy Glorious Coming, Lord."

Your child's graduation? What better time for "It Took a Miracle"?

And when school lets out for the summer and you're faced with three long months of trying to entertain a houseful of adolescents, how about "Where Could I Go"?

When someone cuts in line in front of you at the bank, you might think about breaking into a few choruses of "I Shall Not Be Moved."

A traffic jam? Try singing "I'm Going Through."

A tax audit? How about "That Old Account Was Settled Long Ago"?

And when you rush to take the kids to school in your bathrobe and curlers and run out of gas, you might find comfort in that old favorite "Precious Hiding Place."

The important thing is just to keep a song in your heart. That way, even when a few sour notes do come your way, your walk with him won't miss a beat.

Martha Bolton has been a staff writer for comedian Bob Hope for over fifteen years. She has written more than thirty books, and her *Cafeteria Lady* column in the Focus on the Family teen girls' magazine, *Brio,* has been a favorite with readers since it began. She and her husband, Russ, divide their time between Nashville, Tennessee, and Los Angeles, California.

Look for other books by Martha Bolton!

*To Keep the Love,
Ya Gotta Laugh*

A funny book that talks about marriage from every angle—cooking, gender differences, house hygiene, what those vows really mean, and more.

"A real winner! Martha has stirred together humor with practical Christian values, coming up with a complete recipe for a delightful devotional. It is different from many others and unique in its presentation of married life. I thoroughly loved it and hated for it to end!"

—**Barbara Johnson,** best-selling author

ISBN 0-8007-1774-0
256 pages
$14.99

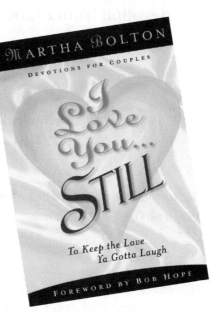

Sample devotion from *I Love You . . . Still*:

1

I've Grown Accustomed to Your Clutter

Be ye kind one to another, tenderhearted, forgiving one another, even as God for Christ's sake hath forgiven you.

Ephesians 4:32

THEY say opposites attract. It must be true because when it comes to clutter, my husband and I are like night and day. I'm one of those people who has a hard time throwing things away. My husband is the exact opposite. He throws *everything* away—broken appliances (a toaster causes *one* lousy kitchen fire and it's history), junk mail (in the very week it arrives), and old phone books (for some reason, he thinks the ones listing party lines are outdated). As you can see, the man has a major problem.

I keep *everything*—coupons that expired during the cold war, every paper my sons ever doodled on, and the voter's pamphlet from the '88 election.

Nowhere is this difference between us more evident than in the bedroom. On my husband's nightstand are his Bible, pictures of the family, and some little ceramic houses that remind him of Skid Row, where he worked as a police sergeant.

My side of the bed looks like Skid Row. There are papers, books, magazines, miscellaneous snacks in varying degrees of decomposition, and the files to whatever projects I happen to be working on. There's so much clutter there, if I ever rolled off the bed, my family wouldn't find me for a week. . . .

Don't Wake Me 'til after Lunch!

WITH A GOOD SENSE for the wild and wacky, Martha Bolton offers today's teenagers a collection of forty-three fun commentaries on life, including "Confessions of a Phoneaholic" and "It's Time to Clean Your Bedroom When . . ." Her hilarious capers and outrageous stunts give readers a welcome chance to find their funny sides amid the awkwardness of adolescence. Teens may find they can't stifle their laughter— no matter how hard they try!

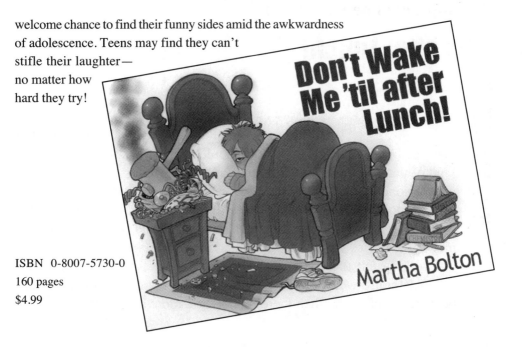

Don't Wake Me 'til after Lunch!

Martha Bolton

ISBN 0-8007-5730-0
160 pages
$4.99

'til after Lunch!

Don't Wake Me

WOULDN'T you like to meet the man or woman who decided school should start in the A.M.? I mean, what kind of person enjoys watching half-awake teenagers show up to class wearing one Reebok and one armadillo bedroom slipper? Does this individual find it amusing when a sleepy-eyed eighth-grader inadvertently starts doing her math assignment with a mascara wand? Or when a drowsy ninth-grader tries sharpening his pencil in the drinking fountain?

I've long felt there would be tremendous advantages to beginning school later in the day. For one thing, a late afternoon history class would be better, because by then there'd be a little more history to study. And evening P.E. classes would be far more popular. In the dark, no one would worry about how they looked in their gym clothes.

Personally, I could have used a later beginning bell when I went to school. You see, I was always a late sleeper. Some mornings the only way to get me out of bed was to put helium in my pajamas. Okay, once I did happen to get up for school on time, but hey, I couldn't count on an earthquake striking *every* morning.

My folks tried to get me to use an alarm clock, but I could never find one I liked. They all made noise when they went off and would wake me up.

But somehow, I always managed to get up, dress, and drag myself to school. I wasn't fully awake until well after noon, though, so my morning classes suffered. The only thing my first-period Spanish class taught me was how to snore in two languages. And I barely passed my second-period sewing class. That's because while everyone else was making blouses, skirts, jumpsuits, and gym bags, all I wanted to make was a pillow. . . .